Apr. 12/97

Dear Alayna
Happy Birthday # 7!

♡ Mrs. MacDonald

Alice and the Birthday Giant

Alice and the Birthday Giant

John F. Green   Maryann Kovalski

North Winds Press

A Division of Scholastic-TAB Publications Ltd.

Cover design: Wycliffe Smith

6 5 4 3 2 1   Printed in Hong Kong   9/8 0 1 2 3 4/9

Canadian Cataloguing in Publication Data

Green, John F. (John Frederick), 1943-
   Alice and the birthday giant

Issued also in French under title: Alice et le cyclope.
ISBN 0-590-73139-4

I. Kovalski, Maryann. II. Title.

PS8563.R416A84 1989   jC813'.54   C89-093343-3
PZ7.G7467Al 1989

This book is for my mother and father.
                                        J.F.G.

The pictures are for Gregory Sheppard,
a giant of a director.
                              M.K.

*A*s usual, Alice had fallen asleep in front of the TV. But this time she woke up feeling especially happy. Today was her birthday and she was going to have a party.

"This is going to be an extraordinary day," she said. "I can just feel it!"

She raced upstairs. But just as she was about to open her bedroom door, she heard something. Someone was snoring, like an outboard motor with hiccups. Alice had never heard anything quite like it before. As quietly as she could, she opened the door.

There, sprawled across her bed, was the biggest, ugliest, messiest looking one-eyed giant imaginable. He was much too large for the bed, which groaned under his weight, and much too wide for the blankets, which would never cover his enormous belly. Every time he snored, the lamp rattled from side to side.

Alice was sure she was dreaming. "Maybe if I close the door and open it again," she thought, "he'll be gone." But as she reached for the doorknob, the giant began to stir in his sleep. His thick, hairy arms almost touched the walls and his legs stuck out over the end of the bed like two huge tree trunks.

"YaaAAWWWwwnnn!" he roared.

Alice jumped right out of the room and slammed the door behind her.

11

When she opened it again, the giant was sitting up, scratching his belly. "Who are you?" he growled.

"My name is Alice and this is *my* bedroom."

"Well, how did *I* get here if it's *your* bedroom," asked the giant, rubbing his head. He fixed his one big eye on Alice. "Do you know anything about that?"

"Not really," she said carefully. "Except . . ."

"Except what?"

"Have you ever wished for something so hard you just knew it was going to come true?" asked Alice. "Yesterday I wished for something very special to happen today, something very big. I think you're it."

The giant snorted. "Well, if you wished me here, then you can just wish me back!"

Alice squeezed her eyes shut and wished as hard as she could. But when she opened them again, he was still sitting there looking worried. "I want to go home," he said.

"I know you do," said Alice, "because if my father catches you he'll have you stuffed and put in a museum."

The giant shivered.

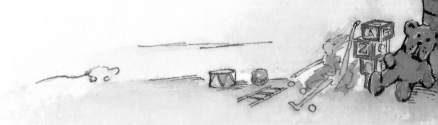

13

"Don't worry, we'll think of something," promised Alice. "But right now I have to get ready for my birthday party. I'll have to find someplace to put you while that's going on."

The giant's eye brightened. "I went to a birthday party once," he cried, smacking his lips. "I ate two hundred and eighty-seven hot dogs and seventy-two bowls of ice cream."

That was all Alice needed to hear. "I'll put you in the storage room," she decided. "Nobody ever goes in there."

She led him through the kitchen and into the basement. "You'll have to keep quiet," she said. "As soon as the party is over I'll figure out what to do with you."

"Promise?"

"Promise," said Alice, and she closed the door.

Alice's father had decorated the kitchen with balloons
and ribbons. The table was covered with paper plates,
pointed hats and horns, hot dogs, pickles and ice cream —
and lots of presents.

Alice's mother was carrying in the biggest, most
scrumptious looking chocolate birthday cake any of them
had ever seen when they heard the sound of thumping
footsteps. Everybody stopped having fun to listen.

Alice's father looked around the table to see if anyone was missing. "Someone is coming up the basement stairs!" he said in amazement.

Alice knew exactly what was happening. "Oh, no," she groaned, "not now!"

All at once the basement door crashed open and flew off its hinges. Scrunched in the doorway, his arms dangling to his knees, his great belly hanging over his belt and his single eye staring at everyone, stood the giant. His bulging nose sniffed the air carefully. "If it isn't too much trouble," he said politely, "could I please have a hot dog and some ice cream?"

For an instant no one moved. Then the entire birthday party went wild. With a screech, Alice's mother sent the birthday cake sailing through the air. It hit the refrigerator door and slid to the floor. Children tripped over one another trying to get out of the way.

They jumped through windows and dived under tables
and chairs. Pickles, hot dogs and ice cream sailed around
the room, splattering the walls and the ceiling. And Alice's
father, his eyes as round as dinner plates, ran right
through the screen door without opening it!

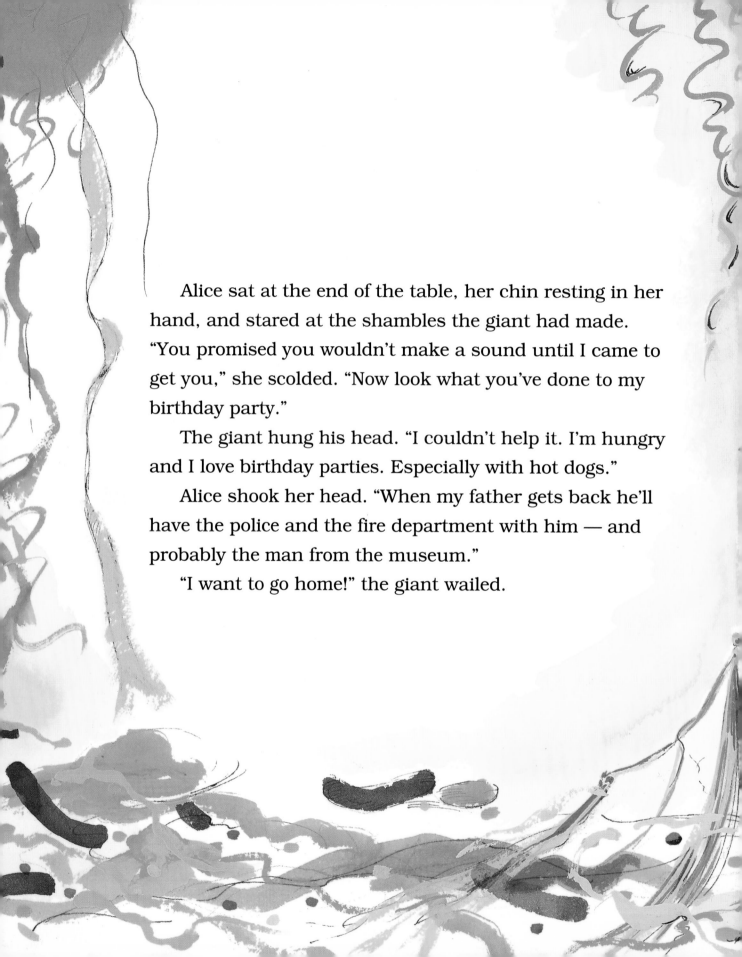

Alice sat at the end of the table, her chin resting in her hand, and stared at the shambles the giant had made. "You promised you wouldn't make a sound until I came to get you," she scolded. "Now look what you've done to my birthday party."

The giant hung his head. "I couldn't help it. I'm hungry and I love birthday parties. Especially with hot dogs."

Alice shook her head. "When my father gets back he'll have the police and the fire department with him — and probably the man from the museum."

"I want to go home!" the giant wailed.

Suddenly Alice was on her feet. "Ms McKracken!" she cried. "She works at the public library. She'll be able to help us."

The giant was already halfway out the door. "What are we waiting for? Hop aboard and point the way."

With Alice high atop his shoulders, the giant strode through the streets toward the library. People scattered in all directions as they approached.

Alice introduced Ms McKracken to the giant. "We need your help to get him home again," she said.

The librarian stared, then frowned at Alice. "What have you been up to?" she asked.

"All I did was make a wish. Honest!"

"It must have been some wish." She looked closely at the giant. "Where did you come from?"

He shrugged his shoulders. "Someplace with mountains, I think."

"That," said Ms McKracken, "could be anywhere."

She moved slowly along the shelves rummaging through books and manuscripts. "There's an old book in here somewhere that's filled with magic spells. I wonder where I've put it?"

The giant was pacing up and down. "I can just see it now," he moaned. "People lining up at the museum doors to see the stuffed one-eyed giant."

"Here it is," Ms McKracken announced, blowing a puff of dust from a very large, very old book.

The giant dug into his pocket and brought out a small eyeglass, which he perched on the end of his nose. He peered at the book curiously as Alice read the title. "*Magic Spells, Witches' Potions and Horrible Oaths.* Isn't that a bit risky?" she asked.

Ms McKracken was thumbing through the book, page by page. "Aha!" she said at last. "Just what we're looking for. A magic spell to make a giant disappear."

"Hold on!" cried the giant. "I don't want to disappear. I just want to get back to — "

It was too late. Ms McKracken had already started the spell.

"Wham bam billy goat,
Simple Simon in a boat,
Spin a giant's head about
And make him disappear!"

The library was suddenly filled with a hundred goats
all in rowboats and all bleating loudly. The giant was
nowhere in sight, but Alice was sure that one of the goats
blinked mournfully at her — with the big round eye in the
middle of its forehead!

31

"Oh, dear, that didn't work at all. I'd better get him back and try again," muttered Ms McKracken.

"Purple bats alley cats,
Thunder lightning rain,
Acrobats floormats,
Bring him back again."

There was a brilliant blue flash and the giant reappeared in the middle of the table. Tiny wisps of gray smoke trickled from his nostrils. Alice thought he looked a bit frazzled. "You're back!" she cried happily.

"Take that book away from her!" the giant yelled. "I can't stand any more of this!"

Just then the library door burst open. In came Alice's father followed by several policemen, the fire chief and a man carrying a very large net.

Alice looked at Ms McKracken. "The next one had better work," she said.

Ms McKracken took a deep breath.

"Forest breeze mighty trees,
Mountains made of stone,
There's a one-eyed giant here,
Please . . . send him home!"

For a few seconds nothing happened. But when Alice turned back to look at the giant, he was gone. A soft wind brushed across her face, and with it came the scent of a mountain valley after a summer rain. It lifted papers, swept through the potted plants and finally disappeared through an open window.

Ms McKracken slammed the book shut. "That," she said firmly, "takes care of that."

35

Alice couldn't believe the giant had left without saying goodbye. She almost wished the spell hadn't worked. She ran past her father, bolted down the steps and raced for home. She flew through the kitchen without stopping to say hello, charged up the stairs and pushed open her bedroom door.

The room was empty. Alice looked under the bed and behind the drapes. She even looked in the closet. The giant was really gone.

"I hope he's gone to a place with lots of birthday parties," she said forlornly. She yawned and stretched out on the bed.

She was almost asleep when she noticed a small round object lying on her pillow. It was the giant's eyeglass, with a note attached to it. The words were written in huge crooked letters:

FOR MY GOOD FRIEND ALICE.

PLEASE KEEP THIS EYEGLASS

TO REMEMBER OUR ADVENTURE.

YOUR FRIEND,

THE GIANT

Alice smiled. Her eyes closed before she read the other side of the note . . .

40